THE MAGIC HORSE

Claudia Casciato

Balboa Press books may be ordered through booksellers or by contacting:

Balboa Press
A Division of Hay House
1663 Liberty Drive
Bloomington, IN 47403
www.balboapress.com
1 (877) 407-4847

Because of the dynamic nature of the Internet, any web addresses or links contained in this book may have changed since publication and may no longer be valid. The views expressed in this work are solely those of the author and do not necessarily reflect the views of the publisher, and the publisher hereby disclaims any responsibility for them.

Any people depicted in stock imagery provided by Thinkstock are models, and such images are being used for illustrative purposes only.
Certain stock imagery © Thinkstock.

ISBN: 978-1-4525-1892-3 (sc)
ISBN: 978-1-4525-1893-0 (e)

Library of Congress Control Number: 2014914162

Printed in the United States of America.

Balboa Press rev. date: 08/12/2014

BALBOA.
PRESS
A DIVISION OF HAY HOUSE

THE MAGIC HORSE

"Yes, you will be a secret agent of God," he explained. "It's time for you to teach others about the healing powers of Heaven."

Chapter 1:

Boom! Boom! Boom! I jumped out of bed to witness the lightning flash through my window. The wind howled. The branches of the tree brushed against the windowpane.

I knelt by my bed and prayed. "Please God, let the thunder stop and help me to get rid of this bad cold. Mary Ellen, my best friend's birthday party is tomorrow."

I picked up the snow globe on my dresser. It was her present. I shook it. All of a sudden I heard a thud in my room. It scared me. I huddled under the bed sheets.

I called out, "Who are you?"

There was no answer. I peeked out. I saw a bubble of green light float in the air.

It burst into a beautiful white horse with gold wings and a black diamond on its' forehead. It flew around me and sat on my bed.

"Be not afraid," said the horse. "I was sent from God."

I was in awe. "Sent from God?"

The horse said, "Your prayer has been answered."

I shook my head. "I don't feel better."

The horse replied, "You must take it one day at a time to heal yourself."

"Heal myself?" I questioned.

"My precious one, you have called upon God to heal you. Healing is like feeling better."

"What do I do to heal?"

"Continue to pray and be patient," said the horse. "Come with me and I will take you to see the other children."

I climbed on the horse though I felt no weight. Like magic, we were in the clouds and came upon golden gates. I walked through the gates. I heard this sweet hymn. I glanced up to witness angels playing the harp. I turned around and saw children in a choir dressed in white gowns. I smelled the perfume of roses.

I was speechless. The horse told me that these children were very ill on Earth and God brought them home. I twirled around and saw massive clouds struck by lightning.

"Why am I here?"

"God wants to show his world."

The choir sang. I felt the words penetrate my heart. I sang the words of the song. It was magical. I felt loved and protected like being cuddled in my mother's arms.

I followed one massive cloud over a field of roses. Raindrops touched my skin but I was dry. It was like God poured love through me. It rained in sheets on the roses. The roses swayed to the music and I swayed to the music. Within me, I felt peace. The magic horse came by my side.

"Come, we must go."

All the children gathered around me and hugged me. They whispered the words: *peace, forgiveness, joy, love and hope.* I wanted to stay but I knew I would miss my family. The magic horse took me home, winked and left. I lied in my bed and hummed the song from Heaven. I turned over and held the snow globe. Before I fell asleep, I heard a voice whisper, "Peace be with you."

The next morning, the birds' chirping woke me up. Their chirping was my alarm clock. The sun peeked through my pink curtains. The rays of the sun touched the chandelier and the room filled with rainbows. I used posters of my favorite singers like wallpaper. My blank canvas was in the corner. The new paintbrushes were untouched.

I thought the horse and Heaven was a dream. I felt my forehead and it was cool to touch. Maybe it wasn't a dream. I remembered it was Mary Ellen's birthday.

I jumped out of bed and sang out, "Happy! Happy! Happy!"

I felt better and ready to go to her party. Mary Ellen was twelve like me.

All of a sudden, I heard barking at my bedroom door, opened it and saw my dog Willie headed for the closet. The magic horse came through the closet door. The barking stopped. Willie jumped on my bed next to me and tilted his head. The magic horse and I laughed.

I said, "What's your name?"

"I'm Raphael."

"I'm Clare," I said. "Willie is my dog."

He said, "It's time for your first assignment."

"My first assignment," I repeated.

"Yes, you will be a secret agent of God," he explained. "It's time for you to teach others about the healing powers of Heaven."

I jumped up and Willie fell off the bed. I giggled.

"Willie does not get it that I will be a secret agent of God."

"Willie is your assistant," he said. "It's time I go and I will see you soon."

He vanished. Willie looked up and around to see where he went. I went to my dresser and picked up my journal. I wrote about my journey to Heaven with Raphael.

I got dressed. I felt shivers down my back as I brushed my curly red hair. Willie barked and I forgot about it.

I picked up my school bag. I jumped two steps down the stairs. As I entered the kitchen, there was complete silence.

I glanced at my mother. Her eyes welled up with tears. My father turned away and gazed at the floor. My mother told me to sit down. I felt like I was chilled to the bone. She sat next to me and took both hands. She cried.

"Mommy, what's wrong?" I asked.

She took a deep breath. "There was an accident."

She explained to me that Mary Ellen got her new bike at the cottage. She rode her bike fast. A car was coming around the corner. It did not stop in time.

I shook. "What happened to Mary Ellen?"

My mother hugged me. "I'm sorry. She went to Heaven."

I erupted like a volcano. "How can you sit here and tell me my best friend went to Heaven?"

She repeated, "I'm sorry."

"You are lying," I said. "She is not dead."

I broke my mother's warm embrace and ran up to my room.

She used white feathers to tickle us. She looked like an angel, her long blonde curls draped over her white dress. The parents relaxed too and joined with the laughter.

Chapter 2:

I picked up the snow globe and shook it with anger. The globe slipped from my hands and smashed on the floor. There were pieces of glass all around me. Sparkles floated in a stream of water.

Raphael appeared and like magic, I saw pieces of glass come together with the sparkles. My mother came into my room. She saw me rock myself on the floor. I held the globe. She cradled me in her arms.

Raphael whispered, "Go to school."

During class, I felt numb. I did not hear my teacher speak. My friends hugged me but I felt cold. I asked to be excused to go to the washroom. I felt weak. The wall held me up till I broke down and cried. I slid to the floor.

All of a sudden I heard the toilet flush and the toilet paper roll. I was alone. I stood up to leave. Raphael appeared.

"Peace be with you."

"I don't understand. Why?"

I twisted around to look in the mirror. I gasped. Mary Ellen stood next to him. I turned around and both of them were gone. I sang the words of Heaven's song and felt at peace.

After dinner, I asked my parents to be excused. I sat on the swing in the backyard. I looked up and saw the swing next to me move. I heard laughter. Mary Ellen appeared and sang our favorite swing song.

"Swing, swing, swing. I love to swing, swing, swing. I love to feel the breeze in the air going through my hair."

I felt like I was six years old again when I met her for the first time at the park. She vanished when my mother came out. She sat on the swing.

"Mom, Mary Ellen came to visit me twice today. First at school and a couple of minutes ago she was here."

"Her funeral is tomorrow," she said. "Would you like to go?"

"Listen to me, she is not dead."

My mother nodded but said nothing. I saw Raphael by the trees. He winked at me.

That night in my bed, I held the globe and shook it. I watched the snowflakes fall.

This is all a dream, I thought. I fell asleep. In the middle of the night, I woke up. I heard laughter. I switched on my lamp and it flickered, then the light went off.

I saw the moon play hide and seek with the shadow of the tree on my walls. I grabbed my pillow tightly. Raphael appeared. The black diamond on his forehead glowed. I stared at it as if I was in a trance. I shut then opened my eyes. He was gone and the lamp came back on.

Suddenly, I heard the children in Heaven sing. I grabbed my journal. The pen flowed as I wrote if I were the one who died, would I want Mary Ellen to come to my funeral? I took three deep breaths and wrote, "Yes". I put my journal away. I gazed at the snow globe till I fell into a deep sleep.

The next morning I woke up to find Willie awake next to me. I got up and opened the closet door. I asked myself what should I wear to my best friend's funeral? I pulled a few dresses. I laid them on my bed. I decided to wear a black dress and matched it up with pink shoes.

I viewed myself in the mirror. I hoped Mary Ellen approved of my funeral dress.

I twirled around with the snow globe and thought how one moment she was on Earth and another moment she was in Heaven.

Before I left for the funeral, I put her birthday card in my pink purse. When we arrived at the funeral, I felt numb and held my parents' hands tightly so I would not faint or fall. I wished Mary Ellen was here. At that moment I felt a light pressure on my head and felt something brush my face. I giggled.

The other children felt the same thing because they giggled too. I saw her. She used white feathers to tickle us. She looked like an angel, her long blonde curls draped over her white dress. The parents relaxed too and joined with the laughter.

At the cemetery, her pink casket was lowered into the ground. Roses of all colors landed on top of her casket. I couldn't breathe. I felt a lump in my throat.

I took her birthday card out of my purse. Something bubbled inside of me. I read her card so everyone heard.

"You are my swing partner. You are my sister and my best friend."

As I read, the tears flowed down my cheeks to the card like raindrops. I kissed her card and threw it on top of the roses. All the children huddled together. Raphael appeared and winked at me.

I thought of the word love and threw the rock. A ruby red crystal appeared in the pond.

Chapter 3:

My First Assignment, Agent Clare

I got ready for bed and prayed. I felt like I was in a dream. None of this stuff made sense. I didn't know what came over me at the funeral. I was the shy one. At school, Mary Ellen defended me when I was teased or someone wanted to pick a fight.

She spoke up for me. Who am I?

I heard Raphael's voice. "You are a child of God?"

"A child of God?" I questioned.

He said, "Children are jewels of God?"

I repeated, "A child of God is a jewel?"

I remembered him say something that puzzled me, my first assignment. Am I ready for this assignment? I was so angry with God for he took my best friend.

He said, "Believe in yourself and you will conquer all."

I was in awe to hear his peaceful voice. I wrote in my journal, "My First Assignment". I took three deep breaths and closed my eyes.

Mary Ellen whispered in my ear. "Peace be with you."

I opened my eyes and Raphael stood by my bed. The black diamond on his forehead switched on like a T.V. screen. I sat up in bed. I saw Mary Ellen's mother drinking. She lied on her daughter's bed.

"Come back, Mary Ellen," she cried. "I can't live without you."

Her mother fell asleep. The diamond switched off.

He said, "Teach her to love again. Teach her that her daughter is here in spirit."

He told me that Mary Ellen and Willie were my assistants in this assignment. He vanished.

I wrote in my journal, Mary Ellen, I miss you. Let me know you are here. Suddenly the dresser shook and I saw snowflakes fall in the globe. I closed the journal and fell asleep.

The next morning I woke up and felt something brush my forehead. It tickled. Mary Ellen appeared. She sat on my bed and twirled her blonde curls with the tip of a white feather.

"I don't get it," I said. "What are you doing here on Earth when you should be in Heaven with the other children?"

She took my hand and placed it on her chest. "I have not completed my assignment here. I want to spend more time with you."

She vanished. I looked in the mirror. Why did I get this assignment? I don't know anything.

I heard Raphael whisper, "Believe in yourself and you will conquer all."

I stood tall and looked at my reflection in the mirror.

I said out loud, "I am a secret agent of God."

I went downstairs to the kitchen. I sat there and played with my breakfast.

"Clare, what are you thinking?" said my mother, as she washed the dishes.

I said, "Mary Ellen is not dead. She is in another world."

She said, "Stop it! I can't understand why you can't accept her death?"

"Mom," I cried, "I love you but one day you will believe with your heart."

She walked over to me and sat next to me. She took three deep breaths.

"Your father and I would like you to see a psychologist, to help you cope with her death."

"Believe with your heart!" I screamed. "Why can't you see that I'm telling the truth!"

I ran out of the kitchen and threw myself on my bed. I felt a light pressure touch my head. I looked up. Mary Ellen and Raphael were there. I brushed my tears away on my sleeve. I told them I was ready for my assignment.

I asked, "Raphael, so tell us, how do we help Mary Ellen's mom?"

She said, "Well, I think we should send her flowers."

I checked my piggy bank and counted my change. "I don't have enough money."

She laughed.

I said, "What's so funny?"

She said, "I used to give flowers to my mom all the time."

I was curious. "What kind of allowance did you get?"

She walked to the window and pointed to all the neighbors' flowerbeds. I was shocked. I told her my mother thought it was a wild rabbit pulling out the flowers. She told me that she pulled fewer flowers from our flowerbed. She used to sneak in their neighbors' flowerbeds while they had dinner. She told me she never got caught.

"I don't agree with your idea," I said. "What about baking cookies?"

She said, "I know, double chocolate fudge cookies with marshmallows dipped in chocolate."

I said, "Hey, I thought they are your favorite cookies."

She rubbed her stomach. "I miss eating, especially sweets."

I said, "Fine, I will make the cookies with my mother."

She changed the subject. "What are we going to do today?"

I smiled. "Don't you have any heavenly chores to do?"

She shook her head. "Nope."

"Where did you get those white feathers?"

She smiled. "I pulled them out from Raphael's golden wings. He had a few white feathers mixed in with the gold feathers."

I laughed. "This is what I miss about you, your great sense of humor."

She giggled. "It is fun to be with you."

I asked her if she recalled the children in the choir from Heaven. She told me that she was not allowed to get past the golden gates. She peaked through the gates but she could not see anything. I told her I went through the gates and saw them.

I said, "They gathered around me before I left. They repeated these words, *love* and *peace* but I forgot the rest."

Raphael appeared. "Remember *forgiveness, joy and hope*. Come with me."

17

I climbed on his back with her. From a distance through the clouds we saw a pond. We landed by the pond and saw fish jump out of the water like dolphins.

Exotic birds whistled in the trees. There were twirling pink lily pads in the pond.

There were colorful waterfalls like a rainbow. The water sparkled like diamonds.

I questioned him. "What is this place?"

He said, "Do you recall when I talked about the healing powers of Heaven?"

I replied, "Yes, it was part of my assignment."

He said, "Throw a rock into the pond and think of one of those words the children mentioned in Heaven."

I thought of the word *love* and threw the rock. A ruby red crystal appeared in the pond.

I said, "Wow!"

Mary Ellen was in awe.

He said, "Now, I want you to throw another rock but this time think of a word opposite to love."

In my mind I thought of the word hate and threw the rock. The crystal shattered.

The birds stopped whistling. The fish disappeared with the lily pads. The waterfalls froze to ice.

I said, "I don't understand what this means."

He said, "Throw another rock and think of another word from Heaven."

She said, "What is the point of this exercise?"

I threw another rock and thought of the word *forgiveness.* An aquamarine crystal formed in the pond. The fish reappeared with the twirling lily pads. The birds whistled.

I turned to him. "Yes, I get it."

She said, "Yeah, I kind of get it."

I questioned him. "What is this place?"

He replied, "This is the healing pond of life."

I smiled. "I released my fear of thinking something bad was going to happen."
She said, "Just by thinking you created this magical world."

Chapter 4:

The Healing Pond of Life

"Look!" I pointed at the crystal.

The crystal changed colors as we heard the sweet hymn from Heaven.

She said, "Do you hear music?"

"Yes, it is the music I heard when I visited Heaven," I said. "Isn't that right Raphael?"

Silence. I turned around and he was gone. She danced to the music and I joined in.

She asked, "What are we going to do today?"

I said, "I have an idea, come on."

She followed me at the water edge. I dipped one foot into the water and it tickled.

She said, "What's so funny?"

I told her someone must be under the water. She saw the water was clear. She dipped her foot in the water and it tickled.

Splash! Splash! Splash! The fish surfaced and jumped out doing somersaults in the air.

I splashed in the water. Suddenly I heard the waterfalls roar like a lion. I stepped back and fell in the pond. I stared at the frozen waterfalls. I wanted to see what would happen if I approached the waterfalls. I got up and moved forward.

"Where are you going?"

"What harm would it do to approach the waterfalls?"

We noticed the fish and the birds disappeared. The sky turned to an ugly orange black. The waterfalls continued to roar.

She came into the water when the waterfalls roared louder. "Stop!"

I continued to walk towards the waterfalls. "All my life I never took a chance to be adventurous."

She grabbed my arm to pull me back. "Ah, excuse me, but do you see where I ended up being adventurous."

"Big deal, you rode your bike fast," I said. "Let's do this together."

We held hands as we approached the waterfalls. The crystal in the middle of the pond shook and disappeared.

I trembled. No, no more fear I said to myself. I took three deep breaths and approached the waterfalls. I stood right in front of the waterfalls. I said to myself, release fear to love, release love to freedom.

Everything shook under my feet like there was an earthquake. I could not believe what happened next?

The waterfalls hummed the song from Heaven. The fish reappeared and the birds flew around the pond. The sky turned to a crystal blue.

She looked puzzled. "What did you do?"

I smiled. "I released my fear of thinking something bad was going to happen."

She said, "Just by thinking you created this magical world.

Raphael reappeared. All of a sudden I could no longer feel my legs and hands. I flew with no wings. I felt myself free with no strings attached. I was part of the sky.

"I'm flying!" I said. "Come and join me."

She said, "Great, now there are two fairies."

He smiled. "Do you understand now about the healing pond of life."

She said, "I get it. My mother told me that when she gave birth to me, she was on cloud nine."

He said, "Watch what happens when fear comes back."

There was a dark cloud that approached me. Lightning struck. I panicked and fell into the pond.

She came by my side to see if I was okay. I was dazed and asked what happened.

He explained. "You see how your emotions affect you."

I said, "No, I don't understand."

He said, "The healing pond of life is within you."

I said, "This is unbelievable!"

He said, "You are the one in control of you."

I said, "This is getting very deep."

She nodded to agree with me.

He said, "You have both witnessed how your thoughts can affect the way you feel."

I came to a conclusion. Now I know her mother drowned in her pain. He told us it was time to go. We were back in my room. Willie came into my room and barked at her. She wanted to pat Willie but he went under my sheets.

I giggled. "I need to digest this information."

She giggled too. "I can't digest it since I don't have a stomach."

I wrote in my journal about the healing pond of life. She stared at the blank canvas. I told her I had painter's block. She laughed. My mom called me to let me know dinner was ready.

I said, "You stay here with Willie."

She replied, "You don't trust me at the dinner table."

I said, "Fine, don't start up that you can't eat."

I went downstairs and hummed the song from Heaven.   My mom was happy to see me sing. My father agreed.

"Mom, you made my favorite dish, roasted potatoes and chicken."

Mary Ellen whispered, "Mm, Mm, it sure smells good."

My mom said, "We booked an appointment for you to see the psychologist tomorrow morning."

I stopped eating and slammed my fork down. "Why don't you believe I see Mary Ellen?"

I forgot about her presence till I saw my roasted potatoes moved on my plate.

They looked like bowling balls as they rolled. I closed my eyes and pretended not to hear her voice. I concentrated on the imaginary pond. I picked up the rock. I threw it.

My mom yelled, "What are you doing?"

I opened my eyes and saw a potato smashed against the wall.

"I'm sorry Mom. I didn't mean to do it."

She was so mad. "Go to your room!"

I snapped. "Maybe if I was the one who died, you would believe!"

I ran to my room and picked up the snow globe. I shook it and it slipped from my hands. Mary Ellen caught it. She hugged me.

I said, "I don't want to see a psychologist."

"Maybe it would not be a bad idea after all," she said. "I will come with you."

I smiled. "Thank you for being here. I will go."

My mom came into my room and sat next to me on my bed.

The glass showered around me without touching me. I heard the music from Heaven as the glass came together as one piece and settled on the bookcase like nothing happened.

Chapter 5:

Psychologist 101

My mom said, "I'm sorry. I don't understand what is going on with you."

"Maybe seeing a psychologist is not a bad thing after all."

I stared at the white medical building with black windows as my mother parked the car.

"I don't know about this idea anymore," Mary Ellen said. "I can't see any light from those windows."

She was right, I thought. I closed my eyes. I saw myself at the pond. I threw a rock and felt calm again. I opened my eyes.

We walked into the waiting room of the psychologist's office. My calmness left me. I watched kids cry and scream at the top of their lungs.

I walked over to an empty chair and stared at the painting on the ceiling. It was a picture of a blue sky with white birds. It circled a yellow cloud. I don't understand the meaning of this painting.

All of a sudden I was distracted. A kid scribbled on a piece of paper. He scribbled so fast like the red crayon was a racecar.

My name was called. I walked into this room. The psychologist's desk was like a tower from where I sat. I turned around and saw a tall glass bookcase.

"What is with the yellow walls?" Mary Ellen whispered. "I'm blinded by the light."

I glanced at the walls. There were no paintings. It was like a blank canvas. I looked down. I saw a reflection of my face through the black marble tiles. I heard footsteps and shot up.

The psychologist walked in. He wore a yellow shirt. It matched the walls. His face was round like his glasses. His hair, it looked like grass. It wasn't green but it did not look like it belonged on his head. He sat down behind his desk. He saw my neck stretch like a giraffe to see him. He got up and sat on a chair in front of me.

He cleared his throat. "I'm Dr. Goodall."

I said, "I'm Clare."

He asked, "What would you like to talk about today?"

I said, "I would like to talk about my friend, Mary Ellen."

He looked again at his papers. "So, I read in your file that she visited you even though she is dead. You know once you're dead, you don't come back."

All of a sudden, I rocked on the chair. I erupted like a volcano.

"Do you think I'm making this up? You are like my mother, she doesn't believe me either."

He adjusted his glasses. "Now calm down. Maybe she is like an imaginary friend."

The psychologist rambled on. I was distracted when I saw Mary Ellen was on his head. He shook his head. She found a golf club and ball on his desk and moved it to his head. She placed the golf ball on the turf and swung the club. The ball hit the glass bookcase. I heard this loud crash. I protected my head.

Raphael appeared. The glass showered around me without touching me. I heard the music from Heaven as the glass came together as one piece and settled on the bookcase like nothing happened. I saw beads of sweat run down his face. The turf on his head landed on his desk.

He called his secretary to come in. I followed the secretary back to the waiting room. It was empty. My mother told me everyone left like a herd.

My mother talked to the secretary to book another appointment. Raphael appeared. The black diamond switched on. I saw Dr. Goodall. He cried in his sleeve. The black diamond switched off.

Raphael winked. I tip toed back into his office. The chair creaked as I sat down.

He shot up. I stared into his green eyes.

I cleared my throat. "What's wrong?"

"I can't believe what happened."

My mother called my name and the secretary walked in.

He said, "Clare can stay."

The secretary left and closed the door.

"My son died three years ago, he was nine."

"I'm sorry."

"I closed my heart after he died."

"You know, when you are ready you can reach your son through your heart."

Lifting his eyebrow. "It's real what I saw?"

I nodded. "Believe you saw it with your heart."

He said, "I never told anyone but I stopped believing in God."

I remembered the birds circle the yellow cloud on the ceiling. I got it. The puzzle was complete.

I questioned him. "The yellow cloud on the ceiling is your son?"

"Yes," he said.

I smiled. "I see those birds as angels."

His eyes widened. "Wow, I didn't think of it in this way."

"Now the yellow cloud is in your heart."

"Clare, thank you, you will make a good therapist one day."

"Thank you Dr. Goodall."

"I believe you see Mary Ellen."

He walked me out. I sat down while my mother talked to him in his office.

Mary Ellen appeared. "What are you thinking about?"

I said, "The healing pond of life gave me a lot of courage.

She said, "Did you like my golf swing?"

I said, "Could you not think of something less dangerous."

She replied, "It was a good golf swing."

Looking at her pouted face. "Yes, it was a swing I will never forget."

We both laughed.

She looked at the ceiling. "I hope I meet his son in Heaven."

I said, "That is if you get through the golden gates."

My mom came out of his office. She looked pale. She took my hand and left. We were in the parking lot. She looked up at the clear blue sky.

She gazed into my eyes. "I believe you."

"You do?"

"Maybe, I have to believe to see."

"What happened in the office?"

"Dr. Goodall made me see the light."

Mary Ellen whispered, "Sure, with those yellow walls anyone can see light."

My heart raced so fast I was out of breath when I reached aisle seven. I saw cascades of chocolates fall on the floor. She sat with her eyes closed in a pond of chocolate.

Chapter 6:

Double Chocolate Trouble

We were on our way home. I told her that I wanted to do something to cheer her mother.

My mom said, "Great, we will pick up flowers at the florist.

Mary Ellen whispered, "Nice mom, she knows best."

I said, "Wait Mom, I have another idea. How about baking cookies?"

She said, "Sounds like a great idea."

I winked with a big grin at Mary Ellen. I explained to her that Mary Ellen loved double chocolate fudge with marshmallows dipped in chocolate cookies.

We made a pit stop at the grocery store. Mary Ellen fixed her eyes at the candy stand as we walked in.

"Get the licorice and chewing gum."

I said, "They are not part of the recipe."

She pouted, "Alright, if only Raphael would make me taste the cookies."

We heard the lady on the loud speaker, "Attention all shoppers, we have a great deal on all chocolates today."

Her eyes widened. "I'm in chocolate Heaven."

I followed her to the chocolate aisle. There was an aroma of chocolate in the air. We saw shelves and shelves of all different types of chocolate. There were chocolate macaroons, fudge, truffles and bonbons packaged from all parts of the world.

My mother yelled, "Clare, where are you!"

I said, "I'm over here, in aisle seven."

My mom laughed. "Okay, pick up the chocolate you need for your recipe and meet me at the cashier line."

I was at the cash register with my mom when I heard a sound like waterfalls.

"Attention, clean up in aisle seven," said the lady on the loud speaker.

My heart raced so fast I was out of breath when I reached aisle seven. I saw cascades of chocolates fall on the floor. She sat with her eyes closed in a pond of chocolate.

I asked, "What are you doing?"

She whispered, "This is my healing pond of life."

I tried to close the flow of chocolate but it was too late for the bags were empty. The pond was full. I closed my eyes as I heard people run towards us. I prayed and felt a breeze go through me.

I opened my eyes to witness a tornado of chocolate being put back into the bags and sealed. The floor was spotless and she disappeared. Raphael appeared and winked at me.

The lady on the loud speaker mumbled, "Attention, disregard clean up in aisle seven. "

I met my mother at the check out counter with another bag of chocolate fudge. Mary Ellen reappeared by the cash register. She pressed a few buttons as the cashier was putting the groceries in the bags.

I said, "What are you doing?"

She said, "I'm pretending to be a cashier like when we used to play store."

Cashier said, "That will be 150.00."

My mother gasped. "Are you sure, I don't see 150.00 worth in my bags?"

Cashier voided the bill and started over again.

She looked puzzled and apologized. "Sorry, that will be 50.00."

My mother sighed. "That's better."

As we walked out of the store to the parking lot, my mother was stumped. She didn't understand how the cashier made a mistake when she saw her key the numbers.

I said, "Maybe, there's a faulty wire in the computer."

She said, "Maybe you're right, sweetheart. Oh, I forgot the marshmallows."

Mary Ellen nudged me. "Check in the bags."

What a surprise. Not one but two packs of marshmallows found.

My mother was puzzled. "I don't recall picking up the marshmallows?"

I changed the subject right away. "I can't wait to make the cookies."

She whispered, "That was fun with the cascade of chocolate."

I said, "The healing pond of life is chocolate?"

She said, "You know, I love chocolate and it does make me happy."

I giggled. "You're right."

When my mother pulled up the car in our driveway, I saw Mary Ellen's mother. She sat on her porch. I got out of the car and went over to her home. Mary Ellen followed me. The wood squeaked under my feet. She had a photo album on her lap.

She smiled and opened her arms. We hugged.

"Stay and look at the photo album with me."

We looked at the photo album three times in silence. She opened the photo album again.

I placed my hand over her hand. "Stop, no more. It hurts me to see her gone too."

She pulled her hand away. "My heart is heavy. I can't let go."

Mary Ellen stood next to me. She placed her hand over her mother's hand. It's like her mother did not feel her. Why am I the only person that can feel her?

I raised my hand and pointed to Mary Ellen. "She is here."

She looked in my direction. "Who?"

"It's your daughter, Mary Ellen."

She lowered her head and opened the photo album again. She pointed at the picture.

"I only see her here."

I repeated. "Open your heart."

She cried. "I can't. I'm so angry with God"

She got up and ran inside like a frightened child. She slammed the door. I walked back home.

Mary Ellen pushed me. "Go back, she needs you."

I turned around to go back to Mary Ellen's home but I stopped. Her mother was too upset to listen to me. I turned around to go home.

I kicked a stone on the sidewalk. "I'm so angry with God."

She hugged me. "It's okay."

"Seeing you in the photo album made me sad again."

"What made me sad is that my mom can't feel me."

I wiped a tear. "I'm sorry. I was only thinking about myself."

She asked, "What do we do now?"

I said, "Let's go make the cookies."

Willie ran towards us with a ball in his mouth. We played with him for hours. I forgot all about the cookies.

From the kitchen window, my mom yelled, "Clare and Willie, supper is ready!"

We laughed as Willie dropped the ball and ran towards the house. I felt like I was being watched. I turned around. Mary Ellen's mother peeked through the window. I stared at her. She shut the blinds quickly.

I sat at the kitchen table. We watched Willie scarf down his food. We laughed.

I said, "Tomorrow is Sunday. Let's make it baking day."

"Sunday will be baking day," she said. "I saw you talking to her mom, is everything okay?"

"I don't want to talk about it. I'm angry with God for taking away my best friend."

I stormed out of the kitchen to my room. I cried myself to sleep.

That night I dreamt I slipped and fell on top of her casket. They shoveled dirt on top of me.

I shouted, "Stop!"

She looked down to view the heart shaped pieces of glass. I bent down to pick up a piece and gave it to her. She placed it between her palms.

She cried in joy. "Mary Ellen is here."

Chapter 7:

Baking With A Twist

I woke up in a sweat. My heart raced. I took three deep breaths to calm down. I picked up the snow globe and shook it. My whole room became a winter wonderland.

Snowflakes fell on my head and bed. I jumped on my bed like it was a trampoline. I felt this surge of energy like I was flying.

Raphael appeared. "She will always be your sister."

I said, "I slipped and fell in my dream because I am a part of her that left Earth."

He winked and the magical wonderland vanished with him. I got up. When I looked out the window. Mary Ellen's room was lit up. How I wish she were here on Earth. I climbed back in bed and fell into a deep sleep.

The next morning I woke up from the aroma of pancakes coming from the kitchen. On the table was a stack of blueberry pancakes with maple syrup cascaded on the sides. A pad of butter melted in a puddle on the top.

I chewed a mouthful of pancakes. "It's baking day."

My mother said, " I don't have a recipe for these cookies."

I was excited, forgot about my pancakes and got up. "Let's create our own recipe. I will get my recipe book."

I pulled my recipe book from my dresser. Mary Ellen appeared.

"I will give you the exact recipe."

"I would like to add other ingredients to make it more my own.

She pouted. "I thought you were going to use my recipe."

Mary Ellen and I could have argued all day but I stood my ground to bake it my way.

"A twist of orange, okay with you?"

She did the twist. "Yah, sounds like a great recipe with a twist."

We both laughed, doing the twist.

As I prepared the ingredients, Willie barked. My mother took him outside. She cracked two eggs in the bowl. The shells became part of the egg white. She fished out the shells with a spoon.

I asked, "What are you doing?"

She replied, "I'm assisting you, sweet heart."

Raphael appeared and watched the process. He shook his head. There was white flour on the floor and clouds of flour in the air. While I used the mixer, chocolate chips flew in every direction. We giggled.

I realized my mom took a long time to come back. He switched the black diamond on. My mom and Mary Ellen's mom chatted at her home by the flowerbed. Willie jumped around on the lawn trying to catch butterflies.

Mary Ellen was so moved. Crash! She dropped a glass bowl. The glass shattered into heart shaped pieces. They shone like diamonds.

We gazed at the pieces. My mother walked in, out of breath and asked what happened? She nearly slipped on the white flour but she grabbed a chair in time.

She gazed down to view the heart shaped pieces of glass. I bent down to pick up a piece and gave it to her. She placed it between her palms.

She cried in joy. "Mary Ellen is here."

I nodded.

"Can I talk to her?

Mary Ellen nodded.

I said, "Yes, you may."

She said, "I'm sorry Mary Ellen, this is new to me to speak to a spirit."

Mary Ellen whispered in my mother's ear. "Peace be with you."

She cried and hugged me. She examined the heart shaped glass.

"How is it possible?"

I said, "Mom, it's okay to not understand right now. We need to help her mother open up her heart."

She said, "I can't do this. I'm having a hard time dealing with Mary Ellen being here."

My mother swayed. I grabbed her arm and pushed her into a chair. I ran to the sink and got her a glass of water.

"Please drink!" I screamed as I thought she was going to faint on me.

She drank the water. "Okay, I feel better. Let's continue to make these cookies."

She went to the counter. There were small balls of cookie dough all lined up on the baking sheet.

She questioned me about whether Mary Ellen was involved with the two bags of marshmallows and the cash register scene.

Mary Ellen waved her hands. "Don't tell her."

I ignored her. "Yes, it was all her doing."

My mother questioned me again whether there was something else I hid from her.

I changed the subject. "These cookies look ready to bake."

The kitchen filled with the aroma of chocolate. She placed the cookies on the rack to cool. She didn't know where to package them.

I snapped my fingers. "I have the perfect idea. I will get my basket."

I rummaged through my closet to search for it. After I finished, it looked like a tornado came through. I sat in a heap of clothes.

Mary Ellen hummed the song from Heaven.

"Sit with me and close your eyes."

I sat next to her on my bed. I closed my eyes. We were back at the healing pond of life. The exotic birds flew around something in the water. They disappeared. The basket floated in the pond.

Once the basket reached the waterfalls, it got caught in a whirlpool. It vanished.

I threw a rock in the pond and thought of the word hope. The basket reappeared. It swirled by the waterfalls and floated back to us. I picked it up. There was a blank note attached to it.

She examined the note. "Why is it blank?"

Something magical happened as we heard the song from Heaven.

Willie barked. I turned around to watch him trying to catch butterflies. He jumped up in the air.

I shouted, "Stop!"

Chapter 8:

Seeing Heaven through the Note

It thundered. Lightning struck. A white feather pen dropped from the sky. It placed itself in Mary Ellen's hand.

The feather pen flowed as she wrote on the blank note.

"I know how much you miss me and I miss you too. You can reach me through prayer and I will come to you. Keep your heart open to receive me in spirit. Be patient for I will meet you when you are ready to accept my death for forgiveness is part of your healing. It's not your fault for you could not stop me to change the path for this is my part to my journey home.

Love you, Sweet Pea"

I opened my eyes. I was alone in my room. The basket was on the dresser with the written note attached to it. I heard the music from Heaven. I felt this peace that not even death can separate us.

I heard my mother call me and woke up from the trance. I picked up the basket and went downstairs to the kitchen.

"There you are. I thought you were outside."

I placed the cookies in the basket. "Is it okay if I go on my own to her home? I know I can help her mother connect with her daughter."

Willie barked. Mom and I laughed.

I said, "No Willie, you cannot have a cookie but you can carry the basket for me."

"I agree with you. Go ahead and help her mom like you helped me open my heart."

I hugged my mom and left. I arrived at her house. I rang the doorbell. No answer. I knocked. Her mom opened the door. She was surprised to see me.

Willie barked. I turned around to watch him trying to catch butterflies. He jumped up in the air.

I shouted, "Stop!"

It was too late. I watched the cookies tumble out of the basket. The cookies formed into a heart sparkling like a diamond in the sun.

Mary Ellen appeared. "You put shiny sprinkles on the cookies."

Her mom cried in joy. "Thank you Clare for the beautiful treat."

"I have a note," I said. "Willie, come here."

Willie came with the empty basket. I took the note and gave it to her.

She cried and read it out loud. She took my hand and placed it on her chest.

"I believe you. I can see with my heart."

She hugged me tightly.

Mary Ellen whispered, "It's my turn to hug my mom."

I said, "Mary Ellen wants to hug you."

She closed her eyes and Mary Ellen hugged her.

She cried, "My baby, I feel you."

Mary Ellen said, "Now I am on cloud nine."

Her mom opened her eyes. "We are both on cloud nine."

"Mom, you can hear me?"

"Yes, I can hear you, sweet pea."

Good work Agent Clare, I thought.

Raphael appeared. "Now are you ready for the second part of your assignment?"

I said, "I thought my assignment was complete."

"It's time to prepare her for Heaven."

"Why can't she stay?"

"Her journey on Earth is finished."

"Please can she stay one more day?"

"Okay, one more day for play."

I heard laughter and turned around. Mary Ellen and her mom sat on the porch. They looked at the photo album.

I said, "This is a perfect picture."

Silence. I turned around. He was gone. Mary Ellen looked at me and blew me a kiss. I walked home with Willie. I turned around to wave to Mary Ellen but she was gone.

He appeared. All of the sudden the snow globe broke in half. My bedroom turned into a winter wonderland. We threw snow at each other. The pink chandelier changed into a solid crystal. It glowed a rainbow of colors like a disco ball.

Chapter 9:

Last Play Day with Mary Ellen

I tossed and turned in my sleep. I woke up in the middle of the night. Flashes of lightning came through my window. Boom! Boom! Boom! I went under the covers. I felt a weight on my bed. I peeked out. Raphael watched me.

"Be not afraid."

"I had a nightmare about losing Willie. He was hit by a car."

"It was only a dream."

"It felt real."

He gazed into my eyes. "You're okay. Willie is okay."

"Mary Ellen is gone. I don't want to lose Willie."

He explained to me that dreaming about a loss is normal. He told me it's okay how I feel. Willie ran into the room and jumped on my bed. I hugged him. I promised Willie I would protect him. I fell back asleep with Willie wrapped in my arms.

The birds chirped away in the morning. The sun came out. I remembered this is the day she leaves for Heaven. Do I tell her? I wrote in my journal – my last day with Mary Ellen. I placed my journal on my dresser next to the globe.

While I brushed my teeth, I saw a reflection of Mary Ellen in the mirror. She sat on the toilet seat.

I said, "It was nice to see that you connected with your mother."

Silence. She walked right in front of me and gazed into my eyes.

"Why are you staring at me?"

"You are hiding something from me?"

I wondered if she could read my mind.

She placed her hand on my chest. "I can read your heart."

"Wow, so what does my heart say?"

"You have a secret and you are not ready to tell me."

While I stood there shocked, the toothbrush dropped out of my hand.

I mumbled. "You're right."

She imitated my voice. "You are my sister and best friend."

"I wrote it in your birthday card."

"Well, I'm waiting best friend."

I took a deep breath. "Today is your last day on Earth."

She viewed herself in the mirror. "I knew something was up because I feel I'm getting weaker."

My chest tightened, like I don't want to part from her. I told her in spirit she will always be connected with us.

She said, "I hope there is a visitor pass to Earth."

I replied, "I hope there is a visitor pass to Heaven."

We hugged each other. We played with Willie in the yard. We swung together and sang our swing song. In the evening before bed I showed her my journal and wrote in it the day we shared together. I wondered if Raphael changed his mind to give us more time to spend together.

He appeared. All of the sudden the snow globe broke in half. My bedroom turned into a winter wonderland. We threw snow at each other. The chandelier changed into a solid crystal. It glowed a rainbow of colors like a disco ball. We made snow angels, held hands and looked up at the crystal.

Tears rolled down my cheeks. I turned my head to look at her. Her hair and face were covered in snowflakes. I saw a glow on her face. Her body radiated this white light.

I knew it was time for her to go.

He said, "Mary Ellen, are you ready?"

She winked at me. "I love you my beautiful sister."

He switched the black diamond. The choir from Heaven sang. The roses swayed.

The lightning touched one of the roses. The rose petals fell. They gathered together and formed her name.

The petals flew as one to the golden gates. The gates opened and two angels were present. The rose petals suspended in mid air like a mistletoe.

The black diamond switched off. My bedroom filled with a green light. A bubble of white light formed around her. The snow globe closed. The crystal broke back into the chandelier.

The snow melted to water and evaporated into a fog. The bubble of white light swirled around me and kissed my face. The fog cleared. She was gone.

He looked at me. "Agent Clare, you have completed your assignment."

I cried. "Where is she?"

The black diamond switched on again. The bubble of white light floated in the clouds. It passed the golden gates and below the rose petals. The rose petals fell on the bubble.

It burst and she was back in the spiritual form again. She walked towards the choir to sing Heaven's song. The black diamond switched off.

I asked, "That's it?"

He said, "That's it what?"

He asked me what other ways to create magic. I closed my eyes. I imagined I was in my room. I picked up the paintbrush to place on my blank canvas. It flowed as I heard the music from Heaven play in my ear. I opened my eyes.

"I can paint what Heaven looks like."

Chapter 10:

I questioned him. "Is that all she does all day as a heavenly chore."

He laughed. "I can't have her picking roses."

I laughed. "Thank you for everything."

He explained to me that she has other heavenly duties.

"Now I must go Agent Clare."

"Wait, don't I get a visitor's pass to Heaven?"

"You don't need one. To get to Heaven, close your eyes and sing Heaven's song. The healing pond of life will take you there."

"So long Raphael."

He vanished. I looked around my room and everything was back to normal. I walked over to my dresser and picked up my journal. I wrote in it about her departure.

I placed my journal on the dresser next to the snow globe. I got in bed and fell asleep.

The next morning I woke up to the aroma of coffee. I walked in the kitchen to hear laughter. Mary Ellen's mom stopped laughing when she saw me. She gave me a big hug.

"I feel peace in my heart. I'm going up to the cottage tomorrow."

"I'm happy you are feeling better."

I walked out to the backyard and sat on the swing. I sang the swing song. All of a sudden the wind pushed the other swing but no sign of Mary Ellen. I heard Willie bark and played with him for hours.

During supper, my mother told me that I had a follow up appointment with Dr. Goodall tomorrow. I was not hungry and played with my food. I asked to be excused and went to my room.

Raphael appeared.

I asked, "Why do I feel so empty? I should be happy for her."

He said, "Don't be sad."

I said, "I miss the magic, Mary Ellen and Heaven."

He said, "Be patient, I have a surprise for you."

He vanished. I picked up my journal and read it.

During the night, I tossed and turned. I heard someone whisper in my ear. I woke up to see Mary Ellen by my closet door. Someone stood behind her. She told me it was Dr. Goodall's son.

"I wanted to let you know we are both okay," she said.

They vanished. The next morning my mother drove me to his office.

When I walked into his room, I was surprised. The yellow walls had paintings. There were live plants. His tall desk was replaced. I didn't have to stretch my neck to see him over his desk.

He wore a green shirt. His turf on his head was gone.

He smiled. "What do you think of my new office?"

I said, "I'm impressed."

He said, "I feel amazing."

I said, "I have good news."

He raised his eyebrow. "Good news?"

I told him that Mary Ellen presented his son to me. He thanked me for sharing. He asked me how I'm coping?

I said, " I feel empty. I feel like I lost something."

He replied, "Lost something?"

I told him a part of me left with Mary Ellen when she went to Heaven.

He said, "It's okay to feel this way. It's not easy to cope with your best friend's death."

I said, "I know, Raphael told me it takes one day at a time to heal."

"Yes, I remember the magic horse," he said. "What is truly going on in your heart?"

I looked down at the floor. "I don't know how to live without her."

He said, "I believe you."

I looked up. "This adventure with her was magical."

He said, "You are afraid the you will not experience this magical adventure again?"

My eyes widened. "Yes!"

"You brought magic back into my life."

"That was all Raphael's work."

He got up. He walked around the room and smiled. He sat down and gazed into my eyes.

"No, it was you that created the magic to open my heart."

He asked me what other ways to create magic. I closed my eyes. I imagined I was in my room. I picked up the paintbrush to place on my blank canvas. It flowed as I heard the music from Heaven play in my ear. I opened my eyes.

"I can paint what Heaven looks like."

He said, "Now you see, you can create magic in your life."

I said, "You are a good therapist."

We both laughed.

He said, "May you have many adventures to explore and tell stories."

I said, "I have a journal where I can write up my magical journey."

Dr. Goodall told me it was time for us to say goodbye.

That night I dreamt about Mary Ellen in Heaven. She worked at the registration desk. As children arrived, she escorted them to the choir. She explained to them in Heaven everyone had an angelic voice. I watched some children tend the rose garden.

She had an argument with Raphael. She wanted to tend the rose garden. A black cloud appeared over her and lightning struck three times. She was back behind the desk.

The next morning I heard the birds chirping. I jumped out of bed and sang, "Hip, Hip, Hooray, it's a beautiful day in every way."

Mary Ellen appeared and sang with me. We held hands and twirled around.

I said, "Did you get a pass to visit me?"

She smiled. "Not exactly, I sneaked out."

There is no way she could sneak out when Raphael could see everything. He must have sent her, I thought. She told me that she hated being at the registration desk.

"At least you have a job in Heaven."

"I'd rather be a cashier on Earth.

I took her hand and lead her to the window.

"You know why you can't tend the garden."

She said, "Why?"

I pointed to all the flowerbeds in the neighborhood. I told her that the flowers she used to bring to her mother belonged to her neighbors not her. She understood.

"I promise never to pick flowers again."

I gazed into her eyes. "I believe you."

Raphael appeared. "Climb on."

We were in the clouds again. From the distance I saw the cemetery where Mary Ellen's pink tombstone came in sight. We held hands and cried.

Suddenly two white doves landed on her tombstone. Like magic, I felt peace. I felt lighter. I saw my feet were off the ground. They watched me.

He nodded and I was back on the ground.

I said, "The emptiness is gone."

He said, "You needed to release your emotions about her death."

I said, " I was busy helping others to heal that I forgot about myself."

He said, " The healing powers of Heaven are in you."

I said, "It will take one day at a time to heal."

He said, "While you are healing, she is healing too."

It makes sense. My spiritual journey does not end here as I looked at her tombstone, it begins here, I thought. All of a sudden, I felt I had a growth spurt.

He must have read my heart. "Maturity does not come with age, only with experiences."

Mary Ellen gazed into my eyes. "We will always be together no matter how far apart we are."

"I agree for two worlds apart will not separate us."

He winked and disappeared. We were alone in the cemetery. We took a walk and found Dr. Goodall son's tombstone. He appeared and stretched his hand to her. She took his hand. It was time to say goodbye to her. They winked at me and vanished.

The sky changed from clear blue to black with lightning. It rained. The sky opened up for the sun came out and used me like a spotlight.

I heard Heaven's choir. The smell of roses perfumed the cemetery. I felt like I was in Heaven for this moment. Everything changed in me for the anger released from me.

Raphael reappeared. "I see you may need a ride to get you home."

"Look at me, I'm happy."

"I see the healing powers of Heaven are working within you."

"I'm very grateful to have you in my life."

"Be not afraid, believe in yourself."

I finished for him. "You will conquer all."

Magic happened. The rain changed to snow in the middle of July. It was a winter wonderland. Every tombstone turned into crystals and hummed the song from Heaven. I heard the waterfalls from a distance.

He nodded and I flew in this paradise. I saw bubbles of white light all around me headed towards the sky. He nodded again and I was back on the ground. The open sky closed and the snow turned back to rain and crystals back to tombstones.

I saw a white rose on the ground and placed it on her pink tombstone. A white dove came, picked up the rose and flew away. It left a petal falling in my hands.

I covered the petal with both hands. When I opened my hands there was a dove. The dove winked at me before it flew away.

I felt my heart open up and heard the words, "Peace be with you, Clare."

I turned to him, "I'm ready for the next chapter on this magical spiritual journey."

The End

Printed in the United States
By Bookmasters